Half a Giraffe

For Cole,
Here's an autograph
for your
"Half a Giraffe"!
Bobby '10

written and illustrated
by
Ryan Kratky

For Denise and Dylan.
I miss you guys.

Deep in the Savanna, among the tall grass
lived a mommy, a daddy, and a baby giraffe.
They lived happily with no problems at all,
except that the baby wasn't very tall.

His mommy was tall and his daddy was tall,
but Baby was short, his neck was so small.

So one day Baby went out on his own,
trying to figure out why his neck hadn't grown.

Suddenly something dropped down from a tree.
"Oh my gosh," cried Baby, "it's a monkey!"

"Nothing," said Baby, "nothing at all.
It's the same as the others, just not very tall."

"Oh," said the monkey, "that's hard to believe. I guess you don't get to have any leaves!"

And the monkey giggled away as he munched, then went back into the tree to finish his lunch.

So Baby walked on, now in a bad mood.
How was he supposed to get any food?

So he walked and walked when suddenly,
he heard a loud squawk from up in a tree.

"It feels great up here,"
he said spreading his wings.
"The sun is one of my favorite things!"

Baby kept walking and thought, 'this isn't fair!
I wanna eat leaves and feel the sun way up there!'

This day of walking was getting quite old,
and Baby was hungry and a little bit cold.

As Baby walked on, he saw one more tree
with a leopard sitting in it looking very scary.

Through his white sharp teeth
growled the leopard,
"Hey you!
From down there
you're missing
an incredible view!"

"There's so much around me
up in this tree.
Down there with you
there's just
not much to see."

Baby, tired of being on the ground all alone, turned around and headed back home.

"Goodbye! Hope you grow!" said his three so-called friends,
as Baby walked home, his trip nearing its end.

And just when he thought that things were so bad,
he saw the tall necks of his mom and his dad.

"Mommy," said Baby with a tear in his eye,
"why are you and Daddy as tall as the sky?"

"Don't worry Baby," said Mommy bent low,
"one of these days, your neck will grow."

And with that, Daddy pulled
a leaf from the tall tree...

...and bent down low to give it to his baby.
And his baby ate it, without one more peep.
"No more worries," said Daddy. "Now go to sleep."

And with his belly full, he laid down in the grass
with the sun shining on his face,
and dreamed he would one day be tall enough
to see all over the place.

Made in the USA
Charleston, SC
10 September 2010